THOMAS & FRIENDS

ANNUAL 2005

Contents

Thomas the Tank Engine & Friends

A BRITT ALLCROFT COMPANY PRODUCTION

Based on The Railway Series by The Rev W Awdry

© Gullane (Thomas) LLC 2004

Photographs © Gullane (Thomas) Limited 2004

Edited by Brenda Apsley and designed by Jeannette O'Toole
Published in Great Britain 2004 by Egmont Books Limited,
239 Kensington High Street, London W8 6SA
Printed in Italy
ISBN 1 4052 1390 6
2 3 4 5 6 7 8 9 10

Hello, _____!

(write your name on the line)

Peep! Welcome to my brand new 2005 annual.

This year is a very special one because it's 60 years since the very first Railway Series stories were written about Edward, Gordon and Henry. You can read one of them, starting on page 32.

I hope you enjoy this year's stories and puzzles. You can read about all your favourite engines, like Percy and James – and me, of course! – and there are some new friends to meet too, like Emily and Arthur.

8

**The
Fat Controller**
is in charge of the railway.

I call **Harold the
Helicopter** "Whirlybird",
because he can fly.

**Henry the Green
Engine** is
engine number 3.

Percy, number 6, is my
special friend. He loves playing
tricks – especially on me!

Annie and **Clarabel**
are my coaches. They
carry my passengers.

Bertie is a bright red
bus. He likes having
races with me.

Bulgy is a grumpy
double-decker
bus.

Emily is new to
Sodor. She's very
kind!

The old blue
number 2 engine is called
Edward.

Gordon, the blue
number 4, pulls the
Big Express.

The red number 5,
James, is a splendid
engine.

Toby is an
old-fashioned
tram engine.

**Terence the
Tractor** is always ready
to help his friends.

Skarloey and **Rheneas**
are best friends who work on
the Mountain Railway together.

Peter Sam is always
ready to do late hours or
extra work.

The Fat Controller
uses **Arthur** to shunt
trucks.

This engine doesn't like
being told what to do.
He's called **Duncan**.

Rusty is a brave little
diesel engine who works
at the Quarry.

Trevor is an
old-fashioned
green traction engine.

Number 27,
Harvey, is a
crane engine.

Now, let's read about them all!

Three cheers for Thomas!

It was a special day on the Island of Sodor.

Thomas had a very important job to do. The Fat Controller had chosen him to take the children to the annual Sports Day.

Annie and Clarabel, Thomas' coaches, were pleased to help. They liked being full of happy, excited children.

Thomas chuffed along to the playing fields and the children all got off. "I hope I win a medal this year," said one of the boys.

"Oh yes," said Thomas. "It must be splendid to win a medal. I'd love to win one."

Thomas wanted to watch the races, but he couldn't, because there was work to be done, so off he chuffed.

Thomas worked hard all afternoon. But he just couldn't stop thinking about winning a medal.

He thought about what it would be like to have a shiny gold medal on a bright red ribbon. How smart he would look! And how proud he would be if it was The Fat Controller who hung it from his funnel!

Later on, Thomas met Percy and Bertie.

"I'm taking The Fat Controller to the Sports Day," whistled Percy.

"Lucky you!" said Thomas. "If you hurry, you can watch the egg and spoon race."

"What?" said Percy. "I didn't know eggs and spoons had races."

"They don't!" said Bertie. "The **children** race, holding spoons with eggs on them."

"Yes," said Thomas. "And the winner gets a medal. Oh, I wish I could win one!"

"Wheesh!" said Percy. "You need to win a race first!"

"I know," said Thomas. "But ... "

"I'll race you, Thomas," said Bertie. "The first one to Wellsworth Station is the winner!"

"You're on, Bertie!" said Thomas.

Ready, Steady, go!

Thomas chuffed off along the railway track, and Bertie hurried along the road.

They both went as fast as their wheels could carry them.

But poor Bertie got stuck behind Trevor, the traction engine, who is very slow.

"Beep!" said Bertie, as Thomas whooshed by.

"Better hurry, Bertie!" shouted Thomas.

When Thomas had to stop to pick up some passengers, it was Bertie's turn to race ahead.

"Better hurry, Thomas!" he called, as he sped across the bridge.

When Bertie had to stop at a level crossing, it was Thomas' turn to race past.

"Last one there puffs hot air!" he called out.

"The Sports Day medals have been left in my office by mistake," he said. **"Will you collect them for me, Thomas?"**

Thomas was still winning the race when he chuffed towards the playing fields.

But when a Signalman waved his flag, he had to stop.

Thomas was cross. **"Peep!"** he said. "Now Bertie is sure to win the race!"

The Fat Controller had asked the Signalman to stop Thomas because he wanted to talk to him.

"Of course, Sir," said Thomas, and off he chuffed.

Thomas forgot all about the race with Bertie. It wasn't as important as making sure the children got their medals.

"I can't let them down ... I can't let them down ..." he puffed as he sped along.

While Thomas was on his way to get the medals, Bertie raced into Wellsworth Station.

"I won!" he shouted. He waited for Thomas to arrive.

But Thomas didn't come ...

Over at the Big Station, the Stationmaster gave Thomas' Driver the box of medals, and Thomas steamed off again, as fast as his wheels would carry him.

He arrived just in time for The Fat Controller to give the medals to the winners.

The next day, there was a big surprise for Thomas. He was having a wash down at the engine sheds, when Bertie arrived with all the children who had won medals at the Sports Day.

The Fat Controller arrived too. "You were very helpful at the Sports Day, Thomas," he said.

"Yes, you were, Thomas, so we've got a medal for you," said one of the boys, and he hung a large gold medal on a red ribbon around Thomas' funnel.

It was a dream come true for Thomas. "My very own medal!" he said. "Oh, thank you."

"Three cheers for Thomas!" said the children. "Hip, hip, hooray!"

Everyone cheered.

"But I still won the race, Thomas," said Bertie.

"Yes, you did," said Thomas, peeping happily. He was much too happy to care about a silly old race!

Spot the difference

Thomas dreamt of winning a medal of his own. How proud he would be if The Fat Controller hung it from his funnel!

1

ANSWERS: 1. Thomas' funnel is taller. 2. The medal ribbon is a different colour. 3. Thomas has an extra lamp. 4. A flag is missing. 5. There is an extra person on the platform. 6. A flag is a different colour.

These two pictures of Thomas look the same, but there are 6 things that are different in picture 2.

Look carefully – can you spot them all?

2

"Peep! Why don't **you** make a wish?
It may come true one day!"

Harold and the flying horse

1. Summer is a very busy time for Harold the helicopter.
There are lots of people who come to the Island of Sodor for their holidays, and Harold spends all day on patrol. He flies around, keeping an eye on things, in case any holidaymakers get in trouble, and need his help.

2. Summer is a busy time for other people, too. Every year the Vicar has a fête, and the engines always like to help.

This year Percy had an important job to do. He was delivering all sorts of things the Vicar needed, like deckchairs, tables and special decorations.

Percy decided to deliver reminders, too. **"Peep!"** he whistled at the passengers. "Don't forget the Vicar's summer fête!"

3. Flying around, Harold looked down on his engine friends. They all had important jobs to do.

When he saw his friend, Thomas, taking an old steam organ to the fête, he felt a bit jealous.

"I'd love to help with the fête," said Harold. "But I can't, because I'm on duty. I have to stay on patrol in case anyone needs my help."

4. Later on, Harold landed at the Airfield because he needed more fuel.

In the next field he saw **Pegasus**, the farmer's big carthorse. He looked splendid!

He was going to the Vicar's fête to give the children rides in his little painted cart.

5. "Even Pegasus is helping with the fête!" said Harold. "Oh, I wish it was me! **I wish** there was some way that I could help, too!"

But he was on duty ...

6. Later, Harold was filling up with fuel when Thomas arrived with some passengers.

"Hello, Harold!" whistled Thomas. "Don't forget the Vicar's fête this afternoon. Everyone will be there."

"Everyone except me," said Harold. "I'm on duty, so I can't go. I have to stay on patrol."

"Oh, I see," said Thomas. "But being a rescue helicopter is a **Really Useful** job, isn't it?"

Harold knew Thomas was right, but he still wished he could help at the fête.

7. Thomas was right about Harold's job being Really Useful, because just then, The Fat Controller arrived in his car with an urgent job for him.

    "Pegasus is stuck in a ditch near Wellsworth," he said. "If he doesn't get to the Vicar's fête, he won't be able to give the children rides, and they'll be very disappointed. Can you rescue him?"

    "I'm on my way, Sir," said Harold, and he took off at once.

8. As he watched Harold fly away, Percy wheeshed loudly. "Pegasus is a funny name for a horse," he said.

    "He was named after a famous horse in an old story," said The Fat Controller. "A flying horse."

    "A flying horse!" said Percy to his Driver. "Horses can't fly. I thought The Fat Controller would know that!" And off he puffed, feeling very clever and pleased with himself.

23

9. When Harold got to Wellsworth, Thomas already had Pegasus' cart on his low-loader.

"What happened?" asked Harold.

"We were loading the cart when poor Pegasus slipped into the ditch," said Thomas. "He can't get out. **He's stuck.** I'll take the cart, but can you rescue Pegasus?"

"Yes," said Harold. "I'll put him in my sling, and lift him out!"

10. Harold's pilot put the sling under Pegasus, then **Harold lifted him gently** into the air, and set off for the fête.

11. When Percy saw Pegasus flying through the air, he was amazed.

"Well, flatten my funnel!" he laughed. **"So horses CAN fly, after all!"**

12. The Vicar's fête was a great success. Pegasus was none the worse for his flight, and he was kept busy all afternoon giving the children rides in his cart. "And it's all thanks to Harold," the Vicar told them.

The children cheered and clapped, and waved to Harold. **"Thank you, Harold!"**

He felt very proud. "I had to stay on duty," he said. "But I helped with the fête, after all!"

Bulgy rides again

You can read this story aloud yourself. There are pictures in place of some of the words, to help you.

 had a problem.

The Fat Controller   Thomas

could not work because he

needed to be mended.

So did  .

Emily

"We need help to carry the

passengers," said  .

The Fat Controller

Then he had an idea, and went to

see  the bus, who was

Bulgy

being used as a house for .

hens

"I'm putting you back on the road," said .

The Fat Controller

"Thank you, Sir," said ,

Bulgy

who soon looked like a new bus!

"We'll start work in the morning," said Bulgy's .

Driver

"You can stay with the hens till then." But when

Bulgy

was asleep, the  crept

hens

onto his luggage racks and went to  !

sleep

They were still there the next

morning, when  picked

Bulgy

up his passengers.

When  got in his way,

Trevor

Bulgy swerved, and the

hens

woke up.

"Squawk!" said the  .

hens

"What's going on?" said Bulgy's

 .

Driver

"Stop!" cried the  .

passengers

"We want to get off!"

"You can still do a job, Bulgy," said  . "The

Emily

farmer

needs a bus to take his

vegetables

around the Island."

Now  has smart new

Bulgy

 paint and a job that

green

he loves.

"You're a Really Useful bus,

 ," said  . "You're

Bulgy

Thomas

a vegetable shop on wheels!"

Odd one out

Look carefully! One picture of Thomas is different from the others. Can you spot the odd one out?

1

2

3

4

ANSWER: Number 3, because his funnel is shorter.

A very special year

Do you know what happened 60 years ago, in 1945?

That was the year when the Reverend Wilbert Awdry wrote his first book. It was called *The Three Railway Engines*, and was about Edward, Gordon and Henry. It had four stories in it, and you can read one of them starting on the next page.

The Reverend Awdry wrote a book about me in 1946, called *Thomas the Tank Engine*, then *James the Red Engine* came out in 1948. Children all over the world loved reading about me and my engine friends, so the Reverend Awdry wrote a new book in his Railway Series every year. Your grandma and grandad and mum and dad read his stories about us – and now you can too!

This is a picture of me in my first book. I looked a bit different, didn't I?

James looked different too. He was black then, but has shiny red paint now!

Edward, Gordon and Henry

Henry thought the rain would spoil his green paint, so he went into a tunnel, and wouldn't come out. The fat director had a wall built in front of him; then he couldn't get out, even though he wanted to.

Edward and Gordon often went through the tunnel where Henry was shut up.

Edward would say, "Peep, peep—hullo!" and Gordon would say, "Poop, poop, poop! Serves you right!"

Poor Henry had no steam to answer; his fire had gone out; soot and dirt from the tunnel roof had spoilt his lovely green paint and red stripes. He was cold and unhappy, and wanted to come out and pull trains too.

Gordon always pulled the express. He was proud of being the only engine strong enough to do it.

There were many heavy coaches, full of important people like the fat director, who had punished Henry.

Gordon was seeing how fast he could go. "Hurry! hurry! hurry!" he panted.

"Trickety-trock, trickety-trock, trickety-trock," said the coaches.

Gordon could see Henry's tunnel in front.

"In a minute," he thought, "I'll poop, poop, poop at Henry, and rush through and out into the open again."

Closer and closer he came—he was almost there, when crack: "Whee——eeshshsh," he was in a cloud of steam, and going slower and slower.

His driver stopped the train.

"What has happened to me?" asked Gordon, "I feel so weak." "You've burst your safety valve," said the driver. "You can't pull the train any more." "Oh, dear," said Gordon. "We were going so nicely, too. … Look at Henry laughing at me." Gordon made a face at Henry, and blew smoke at him.

Everybody got out, and came to see Gordon. "Humph!" said the fat director. "I never liked these big engines—always going wrong; send for another engine at once."

While the guard went to find one, they uncoupled Gordon, and ran him on a siding out of the way.

The only engine left in the shed was Edward.

"I'll come and try," he said.

Gordon saw him coming. "That's no use," he said, "Edward can't pull the train."

Edward puffed and pulled, and pulled and puffed, but he couldn't move the heavy coaches.

"I told you so," said Gordon rudely. "Why not let Henry try?"

"Yes," said the fat director, "I will."

"Will you help pull this train, Henry?" he asked. "Yes," said Henry at once.

So Gordon's driver and fireman lit his fire; some platelayers broke down the wall and put back the rails; and when he had steam up Henry puffed out.

He was dirty, his boiler was black, and he was covered in cobwebs. "Ooh! I'm so stiff! Ooh! I'm so stiff!" he groaned.

"You'd better have a run to ease your joints, and find a turntable," said the fat director kindly.

Henry came back feeling better, and they put him in front.

"Peep, peep," said Edward, "I'm ready."

"Peep, peep, peep," said Henry, "so am I."

"Pull hard; pull hard; pull hard," puffed Edward.

"We'll do it; we'll do it; we'll do it," puffed Henry.

"Pull hard we'll do it. Pull hard we'll do it. Pull hard we'll do it," they puffed together. The heavy coaches jerked and began to move, slowly at first, then faster and faster.

"We've done it together! We've done it together! We've done it together!" said Edward and Henry.

"You've done it, hurray! You've done it, hurray! You've done it, hurray!" sang the coaches.

All the passengers were excited. The fat director leaned out of the window to wave to Edward and Henry; but the train was going so fast that his hat blew off into a field where a goat ate it for his tea.

They never stopped till they came to the big station at the end of the line.

The passengers all got out and said, "Thank you," and the

fat director promised Henry a new coat of paint.

"Would you like blue and red?"

"Yes, please," said Henry, "then I'll be like Edward."

Edward and Henry went home quietly, and on their way they helped Gordon back to the shed.

All three engines are now great friends.

Wasn't Henry pleased when he had his new coat. He is very proud of it, as all good engines are—but he doesn't mind the rain now, because he knows that the best way to keep his paint nice is not to run into tunnels, but to ask his driver to rub him down when the day's work is over.

Eight questions

Can you answer these questions about Thomas and his friends?
All the answers are in this annual.

1. Who is the green number 6 engine?

2. Which engine went into a tunnel, and wouldn't come out again?

3. Which of Thomas' friends can fly?

4. What was the name of the Reverend W. Awdry's first book that came out in 1945?

5. How old is that book in 2005? Is it 60 years old, or 100 years old?

6. Who is the number 1 engine?

7. What are the names of Thomas' coaches?

8. What is the fat director called now?

ANSWERS: 1. Percy. 2. Henry 3. Harold the helicopter. 4. The Three Railway Engines. 5. It is 60 years old. 6. Thomas. 7. Annie and Clarabel. 8. The Fat Controller.

Two the same

Two of these pictures of Thomas are exactly the same. Which ones are they?

1

2

3

4

ANSWER: Numbers 2 and 3, because picture 1 has no number and picture 4 has red buffers.

39

What's the matter with Henry?

It was the end of another busy day on the Island of Sodor.

The engines had worked hard, and they were looking forward to a rest. They were tired, but they had been Really Useful engines, so they were happy.

All except Henry.

He didn't look happy at all. He looked miserable.

He felt ill, and he was very thirsty.

When Henry got to the engine yard, Thomas and Emily were already there.

"Oh, I don't feel well," said Henry. "My poor boiler's grumbling."

Henry often says he feels ill, so Thomas didn't take much notice.

"Cheer up," he said. "I'm sure it's nothing."

Henry looked cross. "It's all right for you to say it's nothing, Thomas," he steamed, chugging slowly away. "It's not your boiler that's grumbling!"

When Henry had gone, Emily saw that he had left a big puddle of water behind him. She felt worried about him ...

"What's the matter with Henry?"

The next morning, The Fat Controller came to the sheds to talk to Thomas, Percy and Henry.

"I want you to collect some trucks from the coaling plant for me," he told them. "I need you to take them to Brendam Docks."

"Yes, Sir!" said Thomas and Percy. They were happy with their jobs, but Henry looked sad.

He didn't feel well, but he knew that Really Useful Engines don't complain, so he didn't tell The Fat Controller how ill he was feeling.

Later on, Henry was on his way to the coaling plant, when Emily steamed by. Henry was leaving water behind him, and she felt even more worried about him.

When Thomas and Percy overtook Henry, cheeky Percy tooted at him. "Hurry up, Henry!"

"I can't go any faster," said Henry.

"Of course you can!" said Thomas. "You're a big, strong engine. **You just don't want to pull those trucks, lazy wheels!"**

Thomas and Percy arrived at the coaling plant to find a long line of trucks waiting there.

"We'll teach Henry a lesson!" Thomas whispered to Percy, and they chuffed off to talk to the manager.

"Please, Sir, Henry wants to take more trucks," said Thomas.

"It's because he's bigger than us," said Percy.

"Very well," said the manager. "You two can take a few trucks each. Leave all the others for Henry."

When Emily got to Brendam Docks, she told The Fat Controller how worried she was about Henry.

When he heard about the water, The Fat Controller was worried about him too. **"He must have a leak,"** he said. "Emily, please go back and make sure he's all right."

"Yes, Sir," said Emily, and she steamed off as fast as she could.

By the time poor Henry got to the coaling plant, Thomas and Percy had gone. There were **lots and lots of heavy trucks** for poor old Henry to pull!

"Oh, no," moaned Henry. "Why did Thomas and Percy leave all these trucks for me? They know I don't feel well."

Henry tried to pull all the trucks, but it was hard work, and he went very slowly.

The trucks were troublesome, as usual, and started to play up. They made fun of Henry.

"Who's out of puff?
Who's in a dream?
Who's got no chuff?
He's out of steam!"

Henry tried as hard as he could, but he just couldn't go any further.

When Emily arrived, he had stopped altogether. "Are you all right, Henry?" she cried.

"No, I'm not," said Henry. "I'm stuck! **I can't move!"**

Poor Henry needed help! His fireman uncoupled the heavy coal trucks, then Emily hooked up to him, and pulled him back to the Docks.

"Wheeesh!" said Henry. "Oh, thank you, Emily."

The Fat Controller was waiting for Henry. "Your pipes are leaking, Henry," he said. "You were very brave, but you shouldn't have been pulling so many trucks."

When they heard, Thomas and Percy felt **ashamed.** They told The Fat Controller what they had done, then they told Henry how sorry they were.

The Fat Controller was not pleased with them. "You two are very naughty engines. You can go back and collect Henry's trucks for him – all of them. **Off you go!"**

Henry went away to be mended, but he was soon back at work, as good as new.

"You look much better, Henry!" said Emily.

"Do I?" said Henry. "Well, the men did mend my pipes, but they didn't even look at my boiler, you know. It's still grumbling. And I've still got my sniffle, and my fuzzy funnel, and ... "

Emily smiled.
"Oh, Henry," she said. "I'm glad to see you're right back to normal!"

Thomas' word puzzle

These words are all from the
What's the matter with Henry? story.

Can you find them in the word square? They are spelled out from top to bottom, and from side to side.

Draw a line around each word when you find it, and tick it on this list.

DOCKS	**STEAM**
PUFF	**ILL**
EMILY	**THOMAS**
SODOR	**PERCY**
HENRY	**TRUCKS**

The answer is at the bottom of the opposite page.

A I P H I L L T
E J E G U O M H
M T R U C K S O
I J C S T E A M
L K Y O Z N P A
Y B W D O C K S
Z Y C O P U F F
H E N R Y X D A

You can read this story yourself. There are pictures in place of some of the words, to help you.

Toby

loves the wooden windmill. It's very old, but Toby's friend, the , still uses

miller

it to make flour.

One day, Toby went to the

windmill

to get some  to take to

flour

the market. But  didn't

Toby

look where he was going, and

he bumped into some  .

trucks

There was  everywhere!

flour

"I may have to shut down the ," said the ,

windmill

miller

as  came to put the

Harvey

trucks back on the track.

That night, there was a storm.

 and  were

Trees

buildings

damaged – and so was the old

! But the

windmill

miller

didn't have any  to

wood

mend it with.

Later, Toby saw a  that

tree

had fallen across the  .

tracks

When The Fat Controller asked

 and  to take it

Harvey   Terence

away,  had an idea.

Toby

"Please, Sir, " he said, "can we

use the  from the tree

wood

to mend the windmill?"

"That's a splendid idea," said

The Fat Controller. "Well done,

 !"

Toby

It took a long time, but at last the windmill was mended. The miller makes more flour than ever, and Toby is proud that the new windmill has a new

name: Toby's Windmill!

Trusty Rusty

1. On the Island of Sodor there is a little railway that twists and turns through the mountains.

It's Rusty's job to look after the line. The little diesel engine and his Driver are kept busy, checking that all the tracks, tunnels and bridges are in good working order.

2. One day, Rusty's Driver checked the supports on the old wooden bridge, and found that there were cracks in them.

"Cracks are dangerous!" said Rusty. "The bridge might fall down if it's not repaired."

"That's right, Rusty," said his Driver. "We must go and warn the other engines. We must tell them not to use the bridge!"

3. Skarloey and Duncan were at the junction when Rusty steamed up.

"You mustn't use the old wooden bridge," Rusty told them. **"It might fall down.** It's not safe."

Duncan wheeshed rudely. "How would you know?" he said. "You're only an old diesel."

And before Rusty could reply, Duncan puffed away, looking **very cross**. He was a fine tank engine, and he wasn't going to let a smoky diesel like Rusty tell him what to do!

4. Rusty set off again. He **raced** down the Mountain Line to tell The Fat Controller about the bridge.

5. "Thank you for warning me about the bridge, Rusty," said The Fat Controller. "I'll send some men to look at it right away. But until they fix it, **no one must use it**, no one."

Rusty's Driver put up a sign to say that the old bridge was not safe, and the engines all went up the mountain on a different track.

6. One day, **Duncan** and **Skarloey** had been working at the Quarry. They were on their way home when Duncan stopped because he needed more coal.

But the coal bunker was empty.

"Where's the nearest bunker, Skarloey?" asked Duncan.

7. "It's on the other side of the old wooden bridge," said Skarloey. "But you can't go across. **The bridge isn't safe.** Rusty said we must not use the bridge."

8. "Hah!" puffed Duncan. "Rusty is such a fusspot. He always makes things sound much worse than they are. What does he know?"

Duncan's Driver agreed with him. "I think it will be all right for us to take one more trip across the old wooden bridge."

"Yes, it's not as dangerous as Rusty says," said Duncan. **"Let's go."**

Duncan steamed quickly onto the old wooden bridge. But when he was halfway across, he hissed, and stopped. He had forgotten that he had run out of coal!

"I've run out of steam!" said Duncan. "I need more coal!"

Just then, Duncan heard a noise. **C-r-a-c-k!**

"What was that?" he asked.

His Driver looked out. "It's the bridge supports!" he said. "The wood is starting to crack!"

CRRRRRAACCCKKK

9. Skarloey was going to get help when he met Rusty. **"It's Duncan!"** he said. "He's gone across the old wooden bridge for coal!"

"Oh, no!" said Rusty. "I told him that bridge is dangerous. I'd better go after him to make sure that he's all right."

CRRRRRAAACCCKK

10. By the time the little diesel engine steamed onto the bridge, the cracks in the wooden supports were much bigger.

As he chugged slowly forward, the track shook and wobbled.

C-r-a-c-k!

Pieces of wood fell off into the river, far below.

CRRRREEEAAAAKK!
CRRRRRAAACCCKK!

"Help!" whistled Duncan. "I'm going to fall in!"

"Hang on," said Rusty. "I'll save you."

11. The Drivers coupled Duncan to Rusty as fast as they could, but the bridge sagged, and Duncan started to slide backwards!

C-r-a-c-k!

"Help!" cried Duncan. "I can't stop! I'm going to fall!"

"Hold on!" called Rusty, and he pulled Duncan clear of the bridge just before it fell to pieces!

SMMAAAASSSSHHH!

12. The Fat Controller was not pleased with Duncan. "You should not have gone across the bridge," he said. "Rusty told you it wasn't safe."

"I know. **I'm sorry, Sir,"** said Duncan. "Thank you for saving me, Rusty. You were very brave."

"Yes, Rusty, you were very brave indeed," said The Fat Controller. "Well done."

Rusty was glad that The Fat Controller was pleased with him. He was so proud that he didn't know what to say!

Colour Thomas and Percy

You can colour your own pictures of Thomas and his friend, Percy! Colour both engines and write what you think they might be saying in the speech bubbles.

Thomas' picture puzzles

Look at the big pictures on these pages. Now look at the little ones, and tick the ones you can see in the big pictures.

peep! Clever you! Well done!

The spotless record

He looked at his stopwatch and smiled. **"You're right on time**, Arthur!" he said. "Well done!"

"Thomas, Percy, this is Arthur, the new engine," said The Fat Controller. "He's here to **shunt trucks** and **pull freight**."

Thomas and Percy looked at Arthur, whose deep red paint shone and sparkled in the sun.

"We are lucky to have Arthur," said The Fat Controller. "He's a fine engine with a spotless record."

It was a very special day for Arthur the big tank engine. He had just come to work on The Fat Controller's railway, and he sped along the tracks as fast as he could. He didn't

want to be late on his first day! He was happy and excited – but he was a little bit nervous too. He hoped The Fat Controller would be pleased with him.

When Arthur stopped at Knapford Station, The Fat Controller was on the platform, waiting for him.

Percy didn't know what that meant. "What's a **spotless record?"** he whispered. "It means he's never done anything wrong," said Thomas.

The Fat Controller sent Arthur to work with Thomas and Percy at the Docks.

Thomas and Percy started bumping the trucks around. They knew it was naughty – but it was **good fun!**

"Come on, Arthur!" said Thomas. **"Bump some trucks** with us. It's fun!"

"No, thank you," said Arthur. He didn't want to spoil his spotless record.

Arthur's first job was to push a train loaded with fruit to the market.

The cheeky trucks sang to Arthur.

**"Root, toot, tow,
We want to go.
The fruit's going off
'Cause you're too slow!"**

"How rude!" huffed Arthur.

The trucks gave Thomas an idea – a **very naughty** idea.

"The Fat Controller doesn't like the trucks to sing, Arthur," said Thomas. "You must stop them."

"I will," said Arthur, as he puffed off along the tracks. "Thank you for telling me, Thomas. I'll keep an eye on them."

"Peep!" said Thomas. "Arthur will be in big trouble if he doesn't let the trucks sing!"

Arthur was chuffing along happily when the trucks started to sing again!

**"Chug, chug, chuff,
You tug and huff,
But you're so rusty
You can't even puff!"**

"No singing!" snapped Arthur. "Thomas warned me about you. I won't be falling for any of your **naughty tricks!"**

The trucks were not pleased. How dare Arthur tell them not to sing! They were **cross**, and they decided to teach Arthur a **lesson ...**

The trucks made things hard for Arthur. They made it very difficult for him to push them. When he had to cross a bridge, he struggled to get the trucks to the other side.

Poor Arthur! How he huffed and puffed!

Arthur was so cross with the trucks that when he got them to the top of a big hill, he was going much too fast, and he sent them rocketing down.

The trucks liked going fast. It made them **laugh** and **giggle.**

But Arthur and the trucks weren't the only ones on the line!

When Arthur's Driver saw a train stopped at the bottom of the hill, he had to put on the brakes.

ssccreeeeeccchhh!

Arthur's wheels skidded on the tracks ...

But it was **too late!**

The trucks smashed into the train, and pineapples, melons and bananas all flew up into the air!

And where do you think they landed? Yes, on Arthur!

SPLAT! SPLOSH! SPLISH!

Yuk! His smart red paint was covered in drips and seeds and squashy bits of fruit.

Poor Arthur! It was his first day, and he had lost his spotless record already!

Arthur was still covered in fruit when Thomas arrived with The Fat Controller.

Now it was his turn to be **cross!** "What happened here?" he asked.

"The trucks were singing," said Arthur. "I told them to stop, and they made me go **too fast!**"

Thomas felt sorry for Arthur. He decided to tell the truth about the trick he had played on him.

"Please, Sir, it's all my fault," said Thomas. "I told Arthur to stop the trucks from singing. It was a **silly thing** to do."

"**Yes, it was,**" said The Fat Controller. "Arthur, you still have your spotless record – and Thomas, you have all this mess to clear up!"

Harvey came with the breakdown crane. He lifted Arthur back onto the track, and Thomas helped the men to clear up all the mess.

It took a **long time ...**

That night, at the sheds, Arthur was having the last bits of squashed melon cleaned out of his funnel when Thomas arrived.

"I'm **sorry** I played a trick on you, Arthur," said Thomas.

"**It's all right,**" said Arthur. "And thank you for owning up, so I didn't lose my spotless record."

Thomas laughed. "Well, **I** never had a spotless record to lose!" he said.

Arthur laughed too.

I think they're going to be **good friends** now, don't you?

Jigsaw pieces

Which little jigsaw pieces complete each big picture?
You can draw them in, if you like!

1

2

3

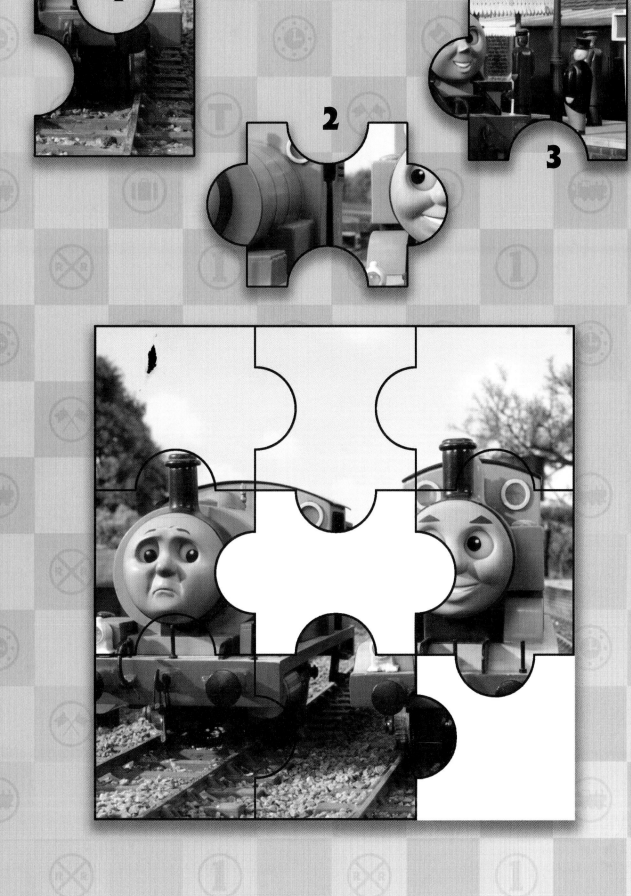

ANSWERS: JIGSAW 1: Pieces 1 and 3. JIGSAW 2: Pieces 1 and 2.

69